THE EXTRAORDINA ORDINARY EVERYTHING ROOM

by

Rhea Tregebov

illustrated by

Hélène Desputeaux

CANADIAN CATALOGUING IN PUBLICATION DATA

Tregebov, Rhea, 1953-
The extraordinary ordinary everything room

ISBN 0-929005-24-4

I. Desputeaux, Hélène. II. Title.

PS8589.R342E93 1991 jC813'.54 C91-093880-6
PZ7.T74Ex 1991

Edited by Peter Carver
Printed and bound in Hong Kong

Published by
SECOND STORY PRESS
760 Bathurst Street
Toronto, Canada
M5S 2R6

Sasha seemed like
an ordinary kid,
but he was the Sasha of
the Everything Room.

Every morning, Sasha's mother walked him all the way to daycare. And every afternoon, his father walked him all the way home.

And every morning and every afternoon, Sasha collected things: shiny marbles and great big soccer balls, crusty leaves and brand new acorns, empty jello boxes and magic wands.

When he got home, Sasha made the leaves into forests and the acorns into forest families. He built castles from the empty boxes. He even cast spells on his father with the magic wand! And when he was done, he put them all away safely in his bedroom to keep them forever.

There got to be so many things, there was just about everything.

And that's why Sasha was the
Sasha of the Everything Room!

The wind was blowing softly when Sasha's friend Daniella from daycare came racing up the stairs.

"Sasha!" shouted Daniella, "my little brother Willy is driving me crazy! It's naptime, but he won't go to sleep unless I play him a sleepy song on his toy saxophone. And his saxophone is broken!

Sasha, do you have a saxophone in your Everything Room?"

"I sure do!" said Sasha. He dug deep into his Everything pocket and took out a key. He put the key in the Everything lock. Then he turned the handle of the Everything door.

Daniella slipped into the Everything Room.
"Here it is!" said Daniella. "I found it — a giant saxophone!"

"Everything's in the Everything Room," said Sasha.

"Thanks, Sasha!" said Daniella, and she gave her friend a kiss.

"You're welcome," Sasha said.

The sun was shining in the windows when Sasha's friend Tai from daycare came galloping up the stairs.

"Sasha!" shouted Tai, "I've played, and I've jumped, and I've climbed, and I've run — and I'm *hungry*! I'm so hungry, I could eat a whole MOUNTAIN of green jello."

"Green jello?" said Sasha, "uuuuchchchch! *Nobody* likes green jello. Yellow jello is best."

"Some like yellow and some like green," said Tai. "It's green jello I want. Do you think we can find some in the Everything Room?"

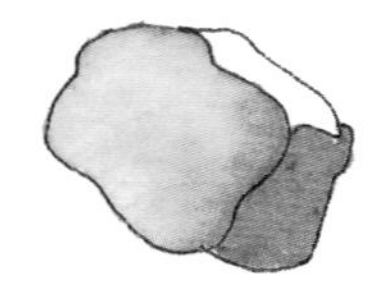

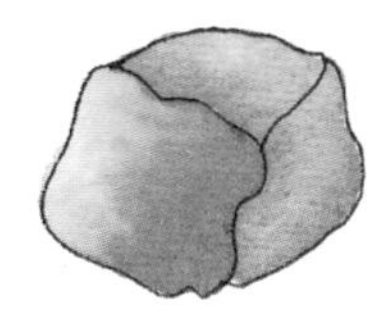

"No problem!" said Sasha. He stuck his right hand down deep into his Everything pocket and took out a key. He put the key in the Everything lock. Then he turned the handle of the Everything door.

Tai wriggled into the Everything Room.

"Here it is!" panted Tai. "Sasha, this is great! Thanks so much."

"It was easy," said Sasha. "Everything's in the Everything Room."

And together they slurped and slogged and woggled the mountain of green jello out of the Everything Room and *ssshhshshshshllooooppp* down the stairs. It sort of slid.

Tai gave his friend a hug.

"Come back soon," Sasha said.

It was a grumbly, grey, BORING day, when Sasha's friend Talia from daycare ran zipping up the stairs.

"Sasha!" shouted Talia, "this is the most boring day that's ever been. Do you think we could find something to fix it in your Everything Room? Something really exciting?"

"Sure we can!" said Sasha. And he reached into his Everything pocket and took out a key. He put the key in the Everything lock. Then he turned the handle of the Everything door.

Talia squeezed into the Everything Room.

For just a moment it was quiet. Then the door burst open ...

and a whole CIRCUS flooded out with jugglers and clowns and tigers and lions and elephants and monkeys and dancing bears and acrobats and poodles-that-could-walk-on-two-legs!

An elephant whisked Talia up onto her back and a juggler started to juggle Sasha's shoes. The bears began to dance with barefoot Sasha. They turned the radio on LOUD!

"This is fantastic!" shouted Sasha and Talia.
"This is the greatest circus ever!"

Acrobats swung from the ceiling lamp. Tigers and lions leaped over and through Sasha's basketball hoop.

Then one clown tried to soak the other with a big bucket of water and Sasha was in the way .... The water ran down his face and splish splash onto the floor. The elephant stomped on Talia's soccer ball, and the monkeys were stealing Sasha's marbles. Then a juggler started juggling Sasha and Talia!

"Th-th-th-this i-i-i-is g-g-g-etting c-c-crazy!" they agreed, and tumbled down.

"Excuse me! EXCUSE ME!" shouted Talia.

But no one paid *any* attention!

"Wait," said Sasha. "I've got what we need in the Everything Room."

When Sasha came back, he had the magic wand in his hand. "This should do the trick.

Hibbidy-hubbidy-hoobidy riot,
try for a minute just being QUIET!"

And one by one, the acrobats, the jugglers, the tigers, and the dancing bears all sat down.

"Please line up," Talia said, "and go back to your places in the Everything Room."

One by one, the clowns, the lions, the monkeys, and the poodles-that-could-walk-on-two-legs all went back to their places in the Everything Room.

Sasha and Talia carefully closed the door. The house was quiet as could be.

Sasha and Talia looked at each other.

"I sort of miss them," Talia said.

"Me too," said Sasha. "But we can always invite them back another day. They're *there.* In the Everything Room."

They both grinned. "Thanks for helping me fix the day, Sasha," said Talia. And she gave her friend a hug *and* a kiss.

“Quite all right,” Sasha said, carefully checking the door.

Later that evening Sasha's mother came slowly up the stairs.

"Sasha," she said, "what is this orange thing on the stairs?"

"It looks like a dancing bear forgot his collar." said Sasha.

"Well, I wish you'd pick up after yourself!" Sasha's mother said, and she sighed.

Then she looked at Sasha.

And then she gave him the biggest hug and the biggest kiss there ever had been.

"What was that for?" asked Sasha.

"I don't know," said Sasha's mother, "just for being an ordinary kid."